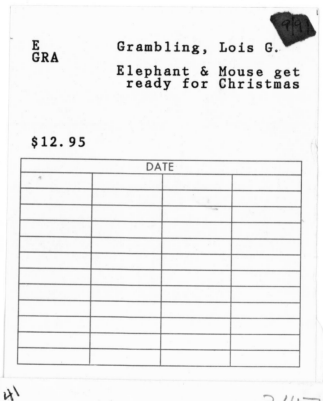

E
GRA

Grambling, Lois G.

Elephant & Mouse get
ready for Christmas

$12.95

DATE			

41

2/47

© THE BAKER & TAYLOR CO.

ELEPHANT & MOUSE
GET READY FOR
CHRISTMAS

by
Lois G. Grambling

Illustrated by Deborah Maze

BARRON'S
New York • London • Toronto • Sydney

For my favorite little Christmas elves
Lara and Tyler

All inquiries should be addressed to:
Barron's Educational Series, Inc.
250 Wireless Boulevard
Hauppauge, NY 11788

International Standard Book No. 0-8120-6185-3

Library of Congress Catalog Card No. 90-755

Library of Congress Cataloging-in-Publication Data

Grambling, Lois G.
  Elephant and Mouse get ready for Christmas/by
Lois G. Grambling.
  32 p.   cm.
  Summary: On Christmas Eve Elephant decides to
switch his huge stocking with the smaller one hung by
his best friend Mouse, so that Mouse will not get fewer
presents.
  ISBN 0-8120-6185-3
  [1. Christmas—Fiction. 2. Elephants—Fiction. 3.
Mice—Fiction.] I. Maze, Deborah ill. II. Title.
PZ7.G7655El   1990
[E]—dc20   90-755
                                             CIP
PRINTED IN HONG KONG   AC

0123   9923   987654321

"It is nice being with your best
friend on Christmas Eve," said Elephant
as he hung a shiny star on the highest
branch of the Christmas tree.
"It is very nice being with your best friend on
Christmas Eve," said Mouse as he hung
some glittering tinsel on the lowest branch
of the Christmas tree.

The two friends stepped
back to admire their tree.
"It is beautiful," said
Elephant. "Really beautiful.
It is the most beautiful
tree in the world!"

"Yes it is," said Mouse, his eyes
bright with happiness.
"Let's hang up our stockings now," said Elephant.
"Let's," said Mouse.
And the two friends walked together into the bedroom.

Elephant opened the top
drawer of the dresser
and took out one of
his stockings.
It was very big.
It was very red.

Mouse opened the bottom
drawer of the dresser
and took out one of
his stockings.
It was very little.
It was very green.

The two friends walked back into the
living room with their stockings and
hung them on the fireplace.
They stepped back to admire them.
"They look very Christmas-y" said Elephant.
"Very Christmas-y," said Mouse.

"Let's read a Christmas story before
we go to bed," said Elephant.
"That would be nice," said Mouse.
"How about *The Night Before Christmas?*"

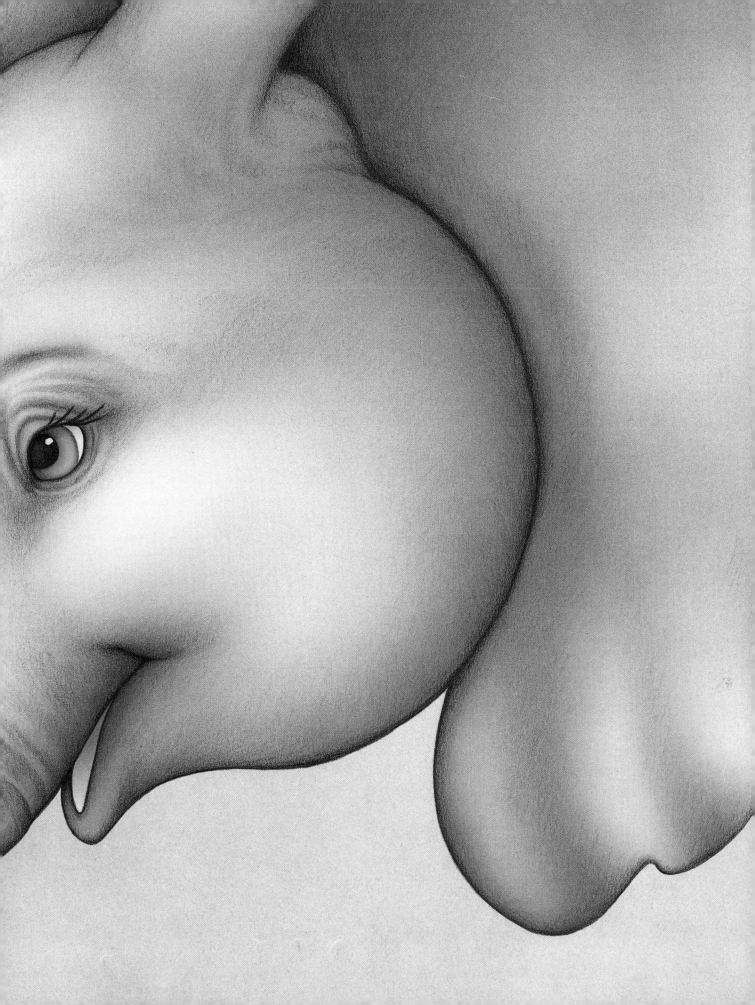

So the two friends sat together in their favorite chair and read *The Night Before Christmas*.

"Let's sing a Christmas song before we put on our pajamas," said Elephant.
"That would be nice, too," said Mouse.
"How about *Jingle Bells*?"
So the two friends sang *Jingle Bells*. Twice.

Humming the last few notes of *Jingle Bells*, Elephant
and Mouse put on their pajamas and climbed into bed.

Mouse fell right asleep.
Elephant didn't.
Something was bothering Elephant.
It was his big red stocking.
It was the "bigness" of his big red stocking.

Every Christmas morning
Elephant's big red stocking
had so much more in it than
Mouse's little green stocking.
This didn't seem to bother Mouse.
But it bothered Elephant.
It bothered Elephant a lot.
And this Christmas Elephant decided
to do something about it.
Elephant had a plan.

Elephant looked over at Mouse.
Mouse was sleeping peacefully.
He had a quiet smile on his face.
And Elephant knew why.
Mouse was dreaming of Christmas morning.

Elephant got out of bed and tiptoed into the living room.
He tiptoed over to the desk and opened the top drawer.
He took out two pieces of paper, a crayon, and two
safety pins.
He wrote MOUSE on one piece of paper and pinned
it to the big red stocking.
He wrote ELEPHANT on the other piece of paper
and pinned it to the little green stocking.

Then he tiptoed back to bed,
closed his eyes
and fell right asleep.
Soon he, too, had a quiet smile
on his face.
Soon he, too, was dreaming of
Christmas morning.

While the two friends slept, the sound of
sleigh bells filled the night sky.
Santa's sleigh came into view.
It landed gently on the rooftop
and Santa got out.

Santa walked over to the chimney.
And started sliding down.
And before you could say
MERRY CHRISTMAS!
He landed thunk kerplunk on the fireplace hearth!

Brushing a bit of soot off his red suit, Santa stepped
out into the living room and looked around.
He saw the Christmas tree.
"Beautiful," he said.
He looked around again.
He saw the big red stocking with MOUSE pinned to it.
He saw the little green stocking with ELEPHANT pinned to it.

Santa scratched his head.
"Something just doesn't seem
right," he said.
Then he chuckled.
"Why, yes, of course!
Now I understand.
Elephant, you rascal!
How fortunate Mouse is to
have a friend like you."

Santa chuckled again.

"Well young fella," he said, his eyes twinkling, "two can play at that game. Especially on Christmas Eve." And Santa took the little green stocking down from the fireplace and tiptoed with it into the bedroom where the two friends were sleeping.

He unpinned the piece of paper from the little
green stocking and put the little green stocking
back in the bottom dresser drawer.
He took a big green stocking out of the top dresser
drawer and tiptoed with it back to the living room.

He hung the big green stocking
on the fireplace, pinned
the piece of paper to it...

and filled BOTH stockings
full to overflowing with
toys from his bag.
"That should do it," said
Santa chuckling again.
"Merry Christmas, Elephant.
Merry Christmas, Mouse,"
he called out softly.

Santa took one last look around
and then
he disappeared up the chimney.

As the sound of sleigh bells
filled the night sky,
Elephant woke up, smiled and whispered,
"Merry Christmas, Mouse."

As the sound of sleigh bells
grew fainter and fainter,
Mouse woke up, smiled and whispered,
"Merry Christmas, Elephant."

Then the two friends closed their eyes and
snuggled back into their dreams of Christmas morning.